Katie McGinty Wants a Pet!

D0551093

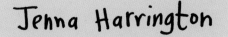

Jenna Harrington

Finn Simpson

LITTLE TIGER PRESS
London

Katie McGinty wanted a pet.
She wanted a pet more than ANYTHING in the world.

She wanted one more than
Tommy Baker wanted to
be a superhero.

More than Millie Phillips
wanted to be able to
stand on her head . . .

. . . and more than Hannah Hobbs
wished she had a sister.

But Daddy told Katie she had
to wait until she was a big girl.
So Katie waited, and measured herself every day . . .

until finally, she WAS big enough!

Katie was so excited she dragged Daddy off to the pet shop. "Slow down, Katie," said Daddy, "and tell me what kind of pet you want."

You have to guess!

"Erm . . .
is it a hamster?"
asked Daddy.

No!

"How about a cat?"
he said.

No!

"...ZEBRA!"

Daddy shook his head in disbelief.
"Sorry, Katie, but you can't have a zebra
as a pet. They **live in Africa** where it's
hot. It's **far too cold** here."

"That's ok, Daddy," said Katie. "Granny can knit him a nice, warm, woolly jumper, and he can wear Mummy's ski boots on his feet."

"Hmm, but you just can't buy zebras in a pet shop," said Dad. "Besides, what would we feed him? We only have a small garden and there's not much grass for him to eat."
Katie shook her head.

"Don't be silly, Daddy!" she giggled. "He'll eat
pizza, and fish fingers, and spaghetti
with us at the table, of course!"

"And I suppose he
would have to sleep
in my shed?"
Daddy asked.

"Don't be silly, Daddy! He's going to sleep in my room in the bunk bed with me," Katie said happily. "In your bunk bed?" Daddy scratched his head.

BLACK BEAUTY

ANIMAL FARM

White Fang

THE JUNGLE BOOK

THE RED PONY

THE CALL OF THE WILD

"And **will** he have a bath with you too?" he asked.
Katie laughed. "Don't be silly, Daddy . . ."

". . . the bath is much too small.

I'll have to wash him at the swimming pool!"

"Katie, we are nearly at the pet shop," said Daddy. "I know you really want a zebra, but I'm afraid you just can't have one."

Don't worry, Daddy! I know I can't have ONE...

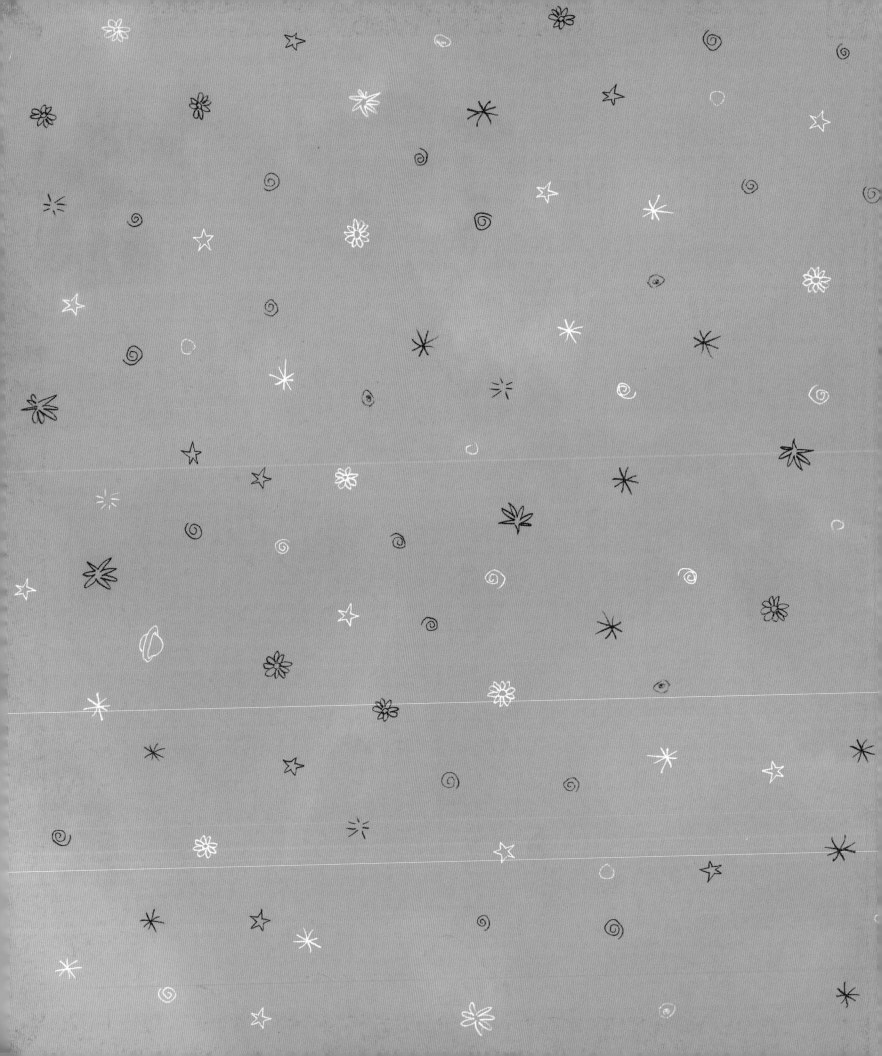